Gwenda Turner
Over on the Farm

THIS BOOK BELONGS TO

_____

Gwenda Turner
Over on the Farm

PUFFIN BOOKS

Over on the farm
in the summer sun
Lived an old mother cow
and her little calf

one

Moo said the mother
We moo said the one
So they mooed all day
in the summer sun.

1

Over on the farm
by the barn painted blue
Lived an old mother sheep
and her little lambs
two

Baa said the mother
We baa said the two
So they bleated all day
by the barn painted blue.

Over on the farm
in the walnut tree
Lived an old mother sparrow
and her little sparrows
three
Chirrup said the mother
We chirrup said the three
So they chirruped all day
in the walnut tree.

1 2 3

Over on the farm
by the farmhouse door
Lived an old mother cat
and her little kittens
four

Miaow said the mother
We miaow said the four
So they miaowed all day
by the farmhouse door.

Over on the farm
where the small fish dive
Lived an old mother frog
and her little tadpoles
five

Swim said the mother
We swim said the five
So they swam all day
where the small fish dive.

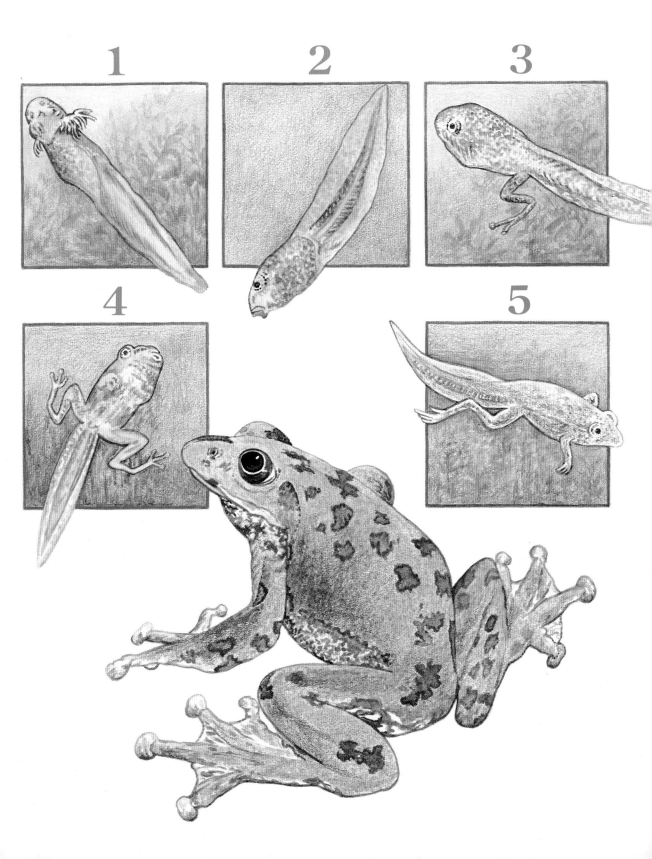

Over on the farm
in a sty built of sticks
Lived an old mother pig
and her little piglets
six

Oink said the mother
We oink said the six
So they oinked all day
in a sty built of sticks.

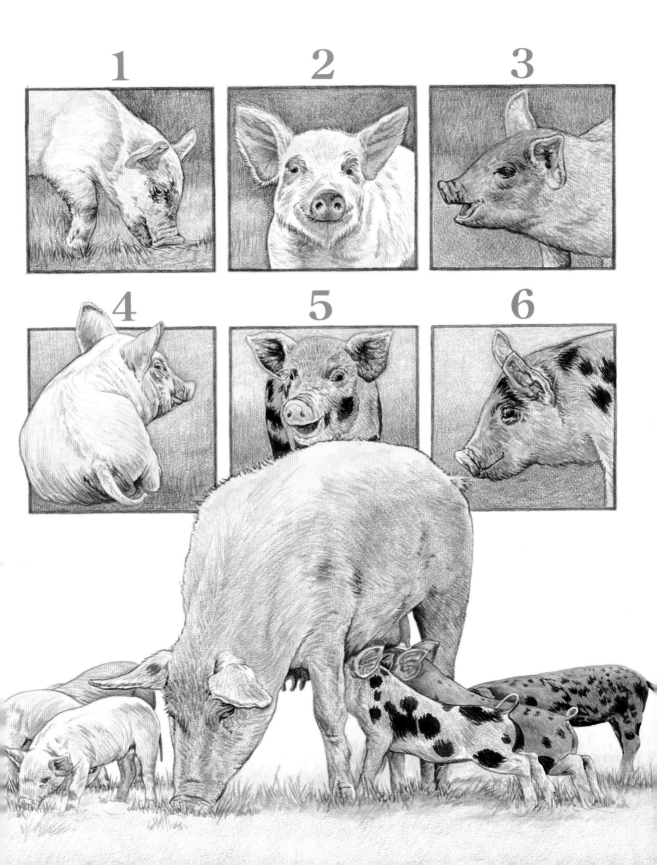

1

2

3

4

5

6

Over on the farm
in a roost named heaven
Lived an old mother hen
and her little chicks

seven

Cheep said the mother
We cheep said the seven
So they cheeped all day
in a roost named heaven.

Over on the farm
by the old wooden gate
Lived an old mother duck
and her little ducklings
eight
Quack said the mother
We quack said the eight
So they quacked all day
by the old wooden gate.

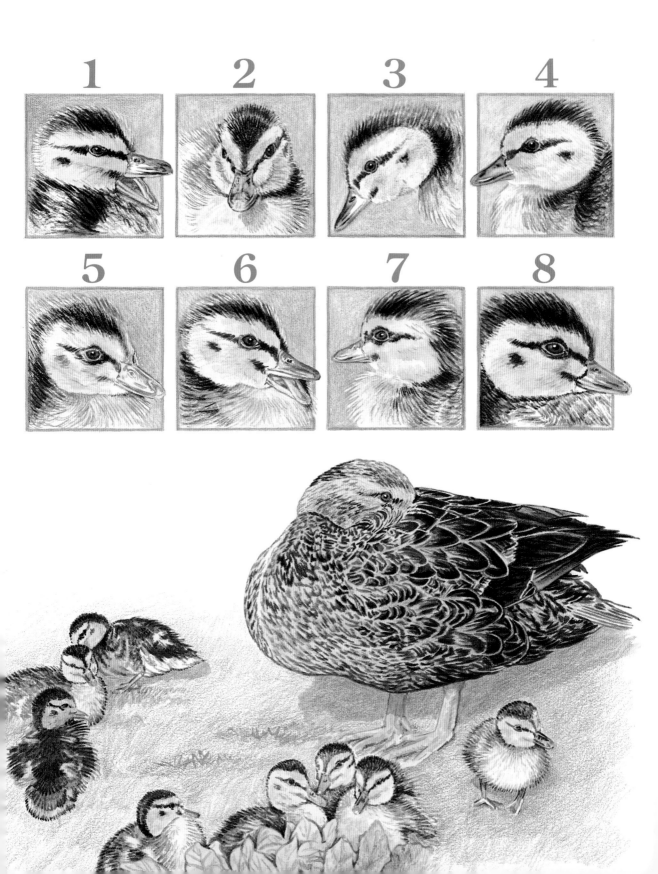

Over on the farm
under the dark green pine
Lived an old mother hedgehog
and her little hedgehogs
nine
Sniff said the mother
We sniff said the nine
So they sniffed all day
under the dark green pine.

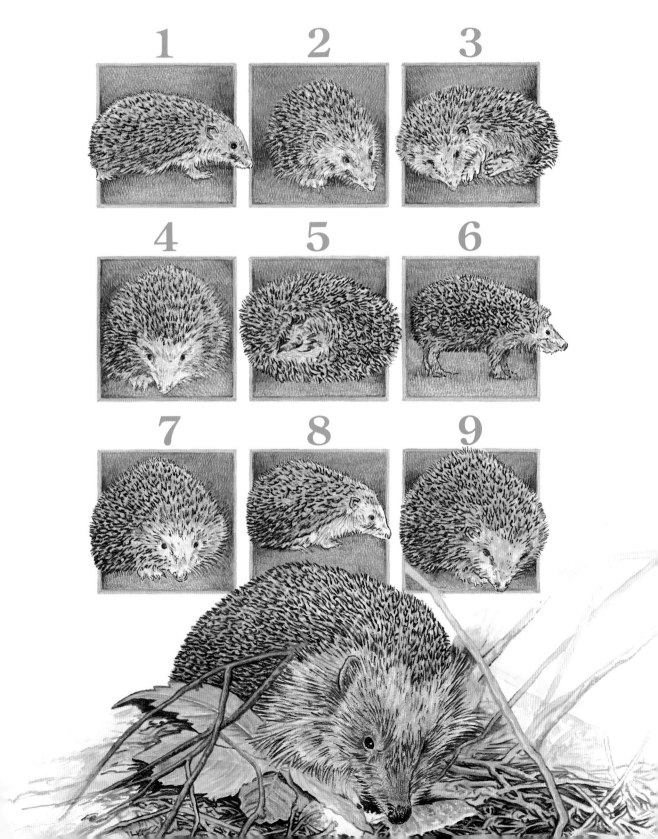

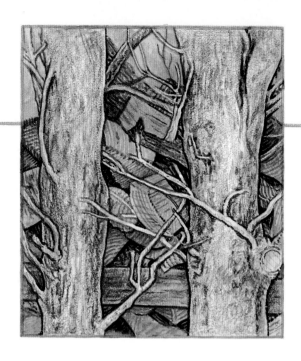

Over on the farm
in a snug wee den
Lived an old mother mouse
and her little mice
ten
Squeak said the mother
We squeak said the ten
So they squeaked all day
in a snug wee den.

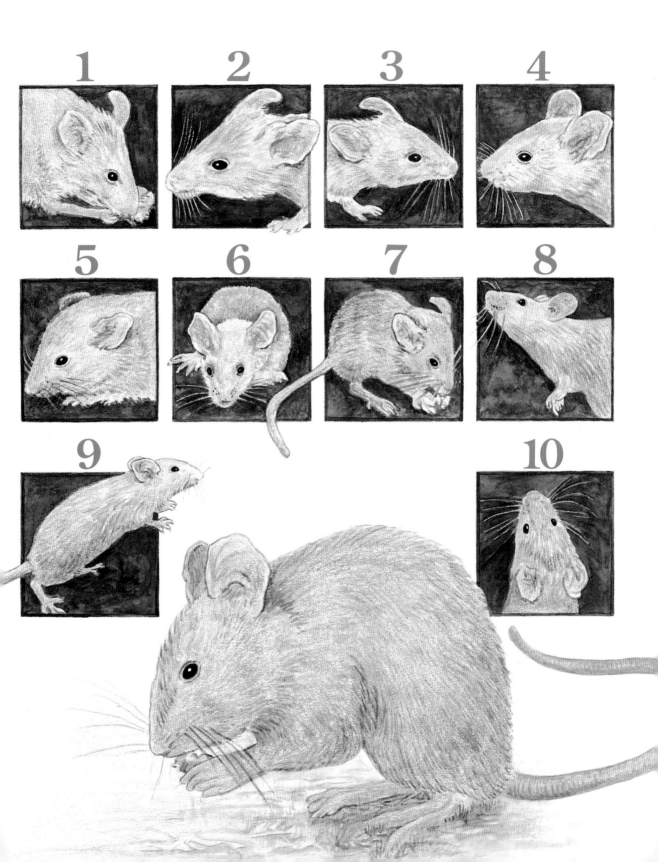

For John

Special thanks to John & Lynda van Beek,
Woolly Meadows Farmyard, Rangiora.

More Books by Gwenda Turner
Once Upon a Time
Shapes
Opposites